W9-CHJ-533

Dear Parent:

Psst . . . you're looking at the Super Secret Weapon of Reading. It's called comics.

STEP INTO READING® COMIC READERS are a perfect step in learning to read. They provide visual cues to the meaning of words and helpfully break out short pieces of dialogue into speech balloons.

Here are some terms commonly associated with comics:
  PANEL: A section of a comic with a box drawn around it.
  CAPTION: Narration that helps set the scene.
  SPEECH BALLOON: A bubble containing dialogue.
  GUTTER: The space between panels.

Tips for reading comics with your child:

- Have your child read the speech balloons while you read the captions.
- Ask your child: What is a character feeling? How can you tell?
- Have your child draw a comic showing what happens after the book is finished.

STEP INTO READING® COMIC READERS are designed to engage and to provide an empowering reading experience. They are also fun. The best-kept secret of comics is that they create lifelong readers. **And that will make you the real hero of the story!**

Jennifer L. Holm and Matthew Holm
Co-creators of the Babymouse and Squish series

Special thanks to Diane Reichenberger, Cindy Ledermann, Jocelyn Morgan, Tanya Mann, Emily Kelly, Sharon Woloszyk, Michelle Cogan, Allison Monterosso, David Wiebe, and ARC Productions.

BARBIE and associated trademarks and trade dress are owned by, and used under license from, Mattel, Inc.
Copyright © 2013 Mattel, Inc. All Rights Reserved.
www.barbie.com
Published in the United States by Random House Children's Books, a division of Random House, Inc., 1745 Broadway, New York, NY 10019, and in Canada by Random House of Canada Limited, Toronto.

Step into Reading, Random House, and the Random House colophon are registered trademarks of Random House, Inc.

Visit us on the Web!
StepIntoReading.com
randomhouse.com/kids

Educators and librarians, for a variety of teaching tools, visit us at RHTeachersLibrarians.com

ISBN 978-0-385-37120-9 (trade) — ISBN 978-0-375-97188-4 (lib. bdg.)

Printed in the United States of America   10 9 8 7 6 5 4 3 2 1

Random House Children's Books supports the First Amendment and celebrates the right to read.

STEP INTO READING®

STEP 3

Barbie
Life in the Dreamhouse

Happy Birthday, Chelsea!

A COMIC READER

Anderson County Library
Anderson, S.C.
IVA

Adapted by Mary Tillworth

Based on the screenplay by David Wiebe

Random House 🏠 New York

It's a special morning.
Barbie, Skipper, and Stacie
are getting ready for
Chelsea's birthday!

Chelsea

It's my birthday. It's finally here!

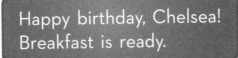

Happy birthday, Chelsea!
Breakfast is ready.

Places, everyone.

We're going to make sure Chelsea's sixth birthday is the best one yet!

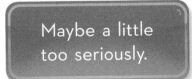
Maybe a little too seriously.

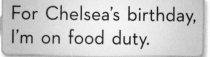

For Chelsea's birthday, I'm on food duty.

Barbie, you're in charge of distracting Chelsea.

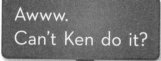

Skipper, you're on decorating duty.

Awww. Can't Ken do it?

Ken's in the garage putting Chelsea's gift together.

It's a bike!

All Chelsea ever talks about is getting a bike.

She is going to be so surprised!

14

The birthday girl appears!

A special birthday breakfast . . .
for a special birthday girl!

18

Meanwhile . . .

Back in the kitchen,
Stacie makes the cake.

Ding!

Baking can be hard work.

And in the living room,
Skipper does the decorating.

Why do I always have the hardest job?

Click!

There are balloons . . .

streamers . . .

and a piñata!

26

28

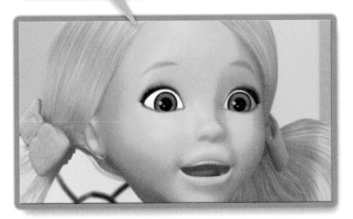

Back in the garage,
Ken has his own problems. . . .

39

The yummy cake . . .

the decorations . . .

the presents . . .

J GRA Tillworth Mary
Tillworth, Mary,
Happy birthday, Chelsea!
22960000868686

NO LONGER PROPERTY OF
ANDERSON COUNTY LIBRARY